ALINE

adapted and illustrated by

P. CRAIG RUSSELL

COLORIST:
LOVERN KINDZIERSKI

LETTERER:
TODD KLEIN

HarperCollins*Publishers*

Library of Congress Catalog Card Number: 2007930658

ISBN 978-0-06-082543-0 (trade bdg.)

ISBN 978-0-06-082544-7 (lib. bdg.)

ISBN 978-0-06-082545-4 (pbk.)

❖

First Edition

I started this for Holly
I finished it for Maddy —N.G.

To Allison, Sloane, and Ivy —P.C.R.

CORALINE DISCOVERED THE DOOR A LITTLE AFTER THEY MOVED INTO THE HOUSE.

IT WAS A VERY OLD HOUSE—IT HAD AN ATTIC UNDER THE ROOF...

...A CELLAR UNDER THE GROUND...

...AND AN OVERGROWN GARDEN WITH HUGE OLD TREES IN IT.

CORALINE'S FAMILY DIDN'T OWN ALL OF THE HOUSE—IT WAS TOO BIG FOR THAT. INSTEAD THEY OWNED PART OF IT.

THERE WERE OTHER PEOPLE WHO LIVED IN THE OLD HOUSE.

THE DAY AFTER THEY MOVED IN, CORALINE WENT EXPLORING.

SHE EXPLORED THE GARDEN. IT WAS A VERY BIG GARDEN. AT THE VERY BACK WAS AN OLD TENNIS COURT, BUT THE NET HAD MOSTLY ROTTED AWAY.

THERE WAS AN OLD ROSE GARDEN FILLED WITH STUNTED, FLYBLOWN ROSEBUSHES...

...A ROCKERY THAT WAS ALL ROCKS...

...AND A FAIRY RING MADE OF SQUIDGY BROWN TOADSTOOLS THAT SMELLED DREADFUL IF YOU TROD ON THEM.

EW.

THERE WAS ALSO A WELL.

CORALINE ALSO EXPLORED FOR ANIMALS. SHE FOUND A HEDGEHOG...

...AND A SNAKESKIN...

...BUT NO SNAKE.

SHE FOUND A ROCK THAT LOOKED JUST LIKE A FROG...

...AND A TOAD THAT LOOKED JUST LIKE A ROCK.

THERE WAS ALSO A HAUGHTY BLACK CAT THAT WATCHED HER...

...BUT SLIPPED AWAY IF EVER SHE WENT OVER TO TRY TO PLAY WITH IT.

CORALINE HAD TO DRESS UP WARM BEFORE GOING OUT EXPLORING, FOR IT WAS A VERY COLD SUMMER THAT YEAR. BUT GO OUT SHE DID, EVERY DAY...

...UNTIL THE RAINS CAME...

...AND SHE HAD TO STAY INSIDE.

MUM, WHAT SHOULD I DO?

READ A BOOK. WATCH A VIDEO. GO AND PESTER MISS SPINK OR MISS FORCIBLE, OR THE CRAZY OLD MAN UPSTAIRS.

I DON'T WANT TO DO THOSE THINGS. I WANT TO *EXPLORE.*

I REALLY DON'T MIND *WHAT* YOU DO AS LONG AS YOU DON'T MAKE A MESS.

CORALINE WATCHED THE RAIN COME DOWN. IT WAS THE KIND OF RAIN THAT MEANT BUSINESS, AND CURRENTLY ITS BUSINESS WAS TURNING THE GARDEN INTO A MUDDY, WET SOUP.

SHE HAD WATCHED ALL THE VIDEOS...

...SHE WAS BORED WITH HER TOYS...

...AND SHE'D READ ALL HER BOOKS.

IT WAS TIME TO VISIT HER FATHER IN HIS STUDY. SHE WALKED DOWN THE HALL.

HELLO, CORA-LINE.

MMPH. IT'S RAIN-ING.

YUP. IT'S BUCKETING DOWN.

NO, IT'S JUST RAINING. CAN I GO OUTSIDE?

WHAT DOES YOUR MOTHER SAY?

SHE SAYS, "YOU'RE NOT GOING OUT IN WEATHER LIKE THAT, CORALINE JONES."

THEN, NO.

SHE DIS-COVERED THE HOT WATER TANK.

tank: in cupboard

SHE COUNTED THE WINDOWS.

tank: in cupboard
21 wind~~o~~

SHE COUNTED THE DOORS.

tank: in cupboard
21 window~~s~~
14 door~~s~~

OF THE DOORS SHE FOUND, THIRTEEN OPENED AND CLOSED.

THE OTHER—THE BIG, CARVED, BROWN WOODEN DOOR AT THE FAR CORNER OF THE DRAWING ROOM—WAS LOCKED.

MUM, WHERE DOES THAT DOOR GO TO?

NO-WHERE, DEAR.

IT **HAS** TO GO SOME-WHERE.

THAT NIGHT HER FATHER MADE DINNER.

IT'S LEEK AND POTATO STEW WITH A TARRAGON GARNISH AND MELTED GRUYÈRE CHEESE.

DADDY, YOU'VE MADE A RECIPE. ICK.

IF YOU TRIED IT, MAYBE YOU'D LIKE IT.

IT'S DISGUST-ING.

THAT NIGHT CORALINE LAY AWAKE IN HER BED. THE RAIN HAD STOPPED AND SHE WAS ALMOST ASLEEP WHEN SOMETHING WENT...

TIK-TIK-TIK-TIK-TIK-TIK

KREEEE...
...EEAAAK☆

DID I DREAM THAT?

SOMETHING MOVED.

IT WAS LITTLE MORE THAN A SHADOW, AND IT SCUTTLED DOWN THE DARKENED HALL FAST, LIKE A LITTLE PATCH OF NIGHT.

SHE HOPED IT WASN'T A SPIDER. SPIDERS MADE HER INTENSELY UNCOMFORTABLE.

THE BLACK SHAPE WENT INTO THE DRAWING ROOM.

SHE FOLLOWED IT A LITTLE NERVOUSLY.

BUT MUM SHUT THIS DOOR, I'M *SURE.*

CLICK

CORALINE WENT BACK TO BED.

SHE DREAMED OF BLACK SHAPES THAT SLID FROM PLACE TO PLACE, AVOIDING THE LIGHT, UNTIL THEY WERE ALL GATHERED TOGETHER UNDER THE MOON. THEIR VOICES WERE HIGH AND WHISPERING AND SLIGHTLY WHINEY. THEY MADE CORALINE FEEL UNCOMFORTABLE.

WE ARE SMALL
BUT WE ARE MANY,
WE ARE MANY
WE ARE SMALL,
WE WERE HERE
BEFORE YOU ROSE,
WE WILL BE HERE
WHEN YOU FALL.

THEN CORALINE DREAMED A FEW COMMERCIALS, AND AFTER THAT SHE DREAMED NOTHING AT ALL.

« 14 »

« 22 »

THE MIST HUNG LIKE BLINDNESS AROUND THE HOUSE. SHE WALKED SLOWLY UP THE STAIRS TO HER FAMILY'S FLAT, AND THEN STOPPED AND LOOKED AROUND.

3

THE NEXT DAY THE SUN SHONE, AND CORALINE'S MOTHER TOOK HER INTO TOWN TO BUY CLOTHES FOR SCHOOL.

THEY DROPPED HER FATHER OFF AT THE RAILWAY STATION. HE WAS GOING INTO THE CITY FOR THE DAY TO SEE SOME PEOPLE.

Brittany's

CORALINE SAW SOME DAY-GLO GREEN GLOVES.

I LIKE THESE A *LOT.*

NO.

BUT MUM, NO- BODY'S GOT GREEN GLOVES AT SCHOOL. I COULD BE THE ONLY ONE.

HER MOTHER IGNORED HER. SHE AND THE SHOP ASSISTANT WERE AGREEING THAT THE BEST KIND OF SWEATER TO GET FOR CORALINE WOULD BE ONE THAT WAS EMBARRASSINGLY LARGE AND BAGGY.

CORALINE WANDERED OFF AND LOOKED AT OTHER DISPLAYS.

OOOOH...

WELLINGTON BOOTS SHAPED LIKE FROGS.

THEN SHE WANDERED BACK.

CORALINE?

OH, THERE YOU ARE.

WHERE ON EARTH WERE YOU?

I WAS KIDNAPPED BY ALIENS FROM OUTER SPACE WITH RAY GUNS...

...BUT I FOOLED THEM BY WEARING A WIG AND TALKING IN A FOREIGN ACCENT...

...AND I ESCAPED.

YES, DEAR. NOW, I THINK YOU COULD DO WITH SOME MORE HAIR CLIPS, DON'T YOU?

NO.

WELL, LET'S SAY A HALF DOZEN, TO BE ON THE SAFE SIDE.

SALE ITEMS

MUM, WHAT'S IN THE EMPTY FLAT?

DO YOU THINK YOU COULD GET INTO IT FROM OUR FLAT?

OH.

NOTHING, I EXPECT. EMPTY ROOMS.

NOT UNLESS YOU CAN WALK THROUGH BRICKS, DEAR.

THEY GOT HOME AROUND LUNCHTIME. IN THE FRIDGE WERE ONLY A SAD LITTLE TOMATO AND A PIECE OF CHEESE WITH GREEN STUFF GROWING ON IT.

I'D BETTER DASH DOWN TO THE SHOPS TO GET SOME FISH FINGERS OR SOMETHING. DO YOU WANT TO COME?

NO.

SUIT YOURSELF.

THEN SHE WENT OUT AGAIN.

CORALINE WAS BORED.

PEOPLE IN DISTANT COUNTRIES

SHE FLIPPED THROUGH A BOOK ABOUT PEOPLE IN A DISTANT COUNTRY; HOW EVERY DAY THEY WOULD TAKE PIECES OF WHITE SILK AND DRAW ON THEM IN WAX, THEN DIP THE SILKS IN DYE, AND THEN FINALLY THROW THE NOW BEAUTIFUL CLOTHES IN A FIRE AND BURN THEM TO ASHES.

IT SEEMED POINTLESS TO CORALINE, BUT SHE HOPED THE PEOPLE ENJOYED IT.

SHE WAS *STILL* BORED.

THE DOOR OPENED ONTO A DARK HALLWAY. IT WAS AS IF THE BRICKS HAD NEVER BEEN THERE.

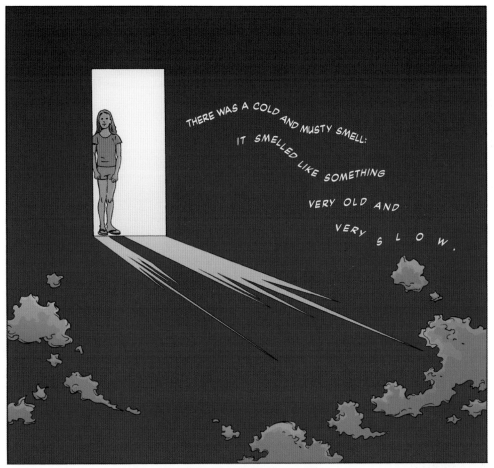

THERE WAS A COLD AND MUSTY SMELL: IT SMELLED LIKE SOMETHING VERY OLD AND VERY S L O W.

CORALINE WENT THROUGH THE DOOR.

IT WAS THE BEST CHICKEN SHE HAD EVER EATEN.

HER MOTHER'S CHICKEN WAS DRY AND TASTELESS, AND HER FATHER DID STRANGE THINGS TO CHICKEN LIKE STUFFING IT WITH PRUNES.

CORALINE WOULD ALWAYS REFUSE TO TOUCH IT ON PRINCIPLE.

SHE TOOK SOME MORE CHICKEN.

I DIDN'T KNOW I HAD ANOTHER MOTHER.

OF COURSE YOU DO.

EVERYONE DOES.

AFTER LUNCH I THOUGHT YOU MIGHT LIKE TO PLAY IN YOUR ROOM WITH THE RATS.

THE RATS?

FROM UPSTAIRS.

CORALINE HAD NEVER SEEN A RAT.

THIS WAS TURNING OUT TO BE A VERY INTERESTING DAY AFTER ALL.

AFTER LUNCH, CORALINE WENT DOWN THE HALL TO HER OTHER BEDROOM. IT WAS DIFFERENT FROM HER BEDROOM AT HOME. FOR A START IT HAD...

PECULIAR SHADES OF PINK AND GREEN.

DON'T THINK I'D WANT TO SLEEP HERE.

STILL...

...IT *IS* A LOT MORE INTERESTING THAN MY OTHER BEDROOM.

THERE WERE ALL SORTS OF REMARKABLE THINGS IN THERE SHE'D NEVER SEEN BEFORE...

WIND-UP ANGELS.

BOOKS WITH MOVING PICTURES.

CHAKKA CHATTA CHATTA CHAK CHAK CHAKKA

HM.

...AND A WHOLE TOY BOX FILLED WITH WONDERFUL TOYS.

THIS IS MORE LIKE IT!

OUTSIDE, THE VIEW WAS THE SAME ONE SHE SAW FROM HER OWN BEDROOM: TREES AND FIELDS AND DISTANT PURPLE HILLS.

HELLO...

...ARE YOU THE RATS?

THEY CAME OUT FROM UNDER THE BED, BLINKING THEIR EYES IN THE LIGHT.

CAN YOU TALK?

THE LARGEST, BLACKEST OF THE RATS SHOOK HIS HEAD.

IT HAD AN UNPLEASANT SORT OF SMILE.

WELL, WHAT *DO* YOU DO?

THE RATS BEGAN TO CLIMB ON TOP OF EACH OTHER, CAREFULLY BUT SWIFTLY, UNTIL THEY HAD FORMED A PYRAMID WITH THE LARGEST RAT ON TOP.

THEN THEY BEGAN TO SING, IN HIGH, WHISPERY VOICES.

WE HAVE TEETH AND WE HAVE TAILS, WE HAVE TAILS, WE HAVE EYES. WE WERE HERE BEFORE YOU FELL, YOU WILL BE HERE WHEN WE RISE.

IT WASN'T A PRETTY SONG. CORALINE WAS SURE SHE'D HEARD IT BEFORE BUT WAS UNABLE TO REMEMBER EXACTLY WHERE.

THEN THE PYRAMID FELL APART...

...AND THE RATS SCAMPERED, FAST AND BLACK, TOWARD THE DOORWAY...

...WHERE THE MAN FROM UPSTAIRS WAS STANDING. THEY SWARMED UP HIM, BURROWING INTO HIS POCKETS, INTO HIS SHIRT, UP HIS TROUSER LEGS, DOWN HIS NECK.

HELLO, CORALINE.

I HEARD YOU WERE HERE. IT IS TIME FOR THE RATS TO HAVE THEIR DINNER. BUT YOU CAN COME UP WITH ME IF YOU LIKE, AND WATCH THEM FEED.

THERE WAS SOMETHING HUNGRY IN THE OLD MAN'S BUTTON EYES THAT MADE CORALINE FEEL UNCOMFORTABLE.

NO, THANK YOU. I'M GOING OUTSIDE TO EXPLORE.

CORALINE COULD HEAR THE RATS WHISPERING TO EACH OTHER. SHE WAS NOT CERTAIN THAT SHE WANTED TO KNOW WHAT THEY WERE SAYING.

THE DOOR WAS OPEN, JUST SLIGHTLY, AND SWUNG OPEN AT HER FIRST KNOCK.

MISS SPINK?

MISS FORCIBLE?

HELLO...?

OH... ...TICKET?

THAT'S WHAT I SAID. *TICKET!*

YOU CAN'T WATCH THE SHOW WITHOUT A TICKET.

TICKET!

CORALINE WALKED OUT OF THE THEATER AND BACK INTO THE GARDEN. SHE HAD TO BLINK HER EYES AT THE DAYLIGHT.

HER OTHER PARENTS WERE WAITING FOR HER.

SO. DO YOU LIKE IT HERE?

DID YOU HAVE A NICE TIME?

I SUPPOSE SO. IT'S MUCH MORE INTERESTING THAN HOME.

I'M GLAD YOU LIKE IT. YOU CAN STAY HERE FOR EVER AND ALWAYS...

...IF YOU LIKE.

HMMM...

SHE PUT HER HAND IN HER POCKET AND THOUGHT ABOUT IT.

HER HAND TOUCHED THE STONE WITH THE HOLE IN IT.

IF YOU WANT TO STAY, THERE'S ONLY ONE LITTLE THING WE'LL HAVE TO DO, SO YOU CAN STAY HERE FOR EVER AND ALWAYS.

THEY WENT INTO THE KITCHEN. ON THE TABLE WAS A SPOOL OF BLACK COTTON, AND A LONG SILVER NEEDLE, AND BESIDE THEM, TWO LARGE BLACK BUTTONS.

CORALINE KNEW THAT WHEN GROWN-UPS TOLD YOU SOMETHING WOULDN'T HURT IT ALMOST ALWAYS DID.

NO!

WE ONLY WANT WHAT'S BEST FOR YOU.

I'M GOING NOW.

HER FINGERS CLOSED AROUND THE STONE WITH THE HOLE IN IT...

...AND HER OTHER MOTHER'S HAND SCUTTLED OFF CORALINE'S SHOULDER LIKE A FRIGHTENED SPIDER.

IF THAT'S WHAT YOU WANT.

YES!

WE'LL SEE YOU SOON, THOUGH, WHEN YOU COME BACK.

AND THEN WE'LL ALL BE TOGETHER AS ONE BIG HAPPY FAMILY...

...FOR EVER AND ALWAYS.

CORALINE HURRIED INTO THE DRAWING ROOM AND HEADED STRAIGHT FOR THE DOOR IN THE CORNER.

THERE WAS NO BRICK WALL THERE NOW—JUST DARKNESS. A DARKNESS THAT SEEMED AS IF THINGS IN IT MIGHT BE MOVING.

COME BACK SOON.

SHE TOOK A DEEP BREATH...

...AND STEPPED INTO THE HOWLING DARKNESS. SHE BECAME CONVINCED THAT THERE WAS SOMETHING VERY OLD AND VERY SLOW IN THE DARK BEHIND HER.

SHE BUMPED INTO SOME-THING...

...AN ARM-CHAIR.

THE DOORWAY BEHIND HER WAS BLOCKED BY ROUGH RED BRICKS.

SHE WAS HOME.

THEN CORALINE WATCHED TELEVISION. SHE WONDERED WHY GROWN-UPS GAVE THEMSELVES ALL THE GOOD PROGRAMS, WITH ALL THE SHOUTING AND RUNNING AROUND IN.

AFTER A WHILE SHE STARTED YAWNING.

THEN SHE UNDRESSED...

...BRUSHED HER TEETH...

...AND PUT HERSELF TO BED.

IN THE MORNING SHE WENT INTO HER PARENTS' ROOM, BUT THEIR BED HADN'T BEEN SLEPT IN, AND THEY WEREN'T AROUND.

SHE ATE CANNED SPAGHETTI FOR BREAKFAST.

FOR LUNCH, A BLOCK OF COOKING CHOCOLATE AND AN APPLE. THE APPLE WAS SLIGHTLY SHRIVELED, BUT IT TASTED SWEET AND GOOD.

FOR TEA SHE WENT DOWN TO SEE MISSES SPINK AND FORCIBLE. SHE HAD THREE DIGESTIVE BISCUITS AND A GLASS OF LIMEADE. IT TASTED BRIGHT GREEN AND VAGUELY CHEMICAL.

SHE LIKED IT ENORMOUSLY.

HOW ARE YOUR DEAR MOTHER AND FATHER?

MISSING. I HAVEN'T SEEN EITHER OF THEM SINCE YESTERDAY. I'M ON MY OWN. I THINK I'VE BECOME A SINGLE CHILD FAMILY.

TELL YOUR MOTHER THAT WE FOUND THE *GLASGOW EMPIRE* PRESS CLIPPINGS WE WERE TELLING HER ABOUT. SHE SEEMED VERY INTERESTED IN THEM.

SHE'S VANISHED UNDER MYSTERIOUS CIRCUMSTANCES, AND I BELIEVE MY FATHER HAS AS WELL.

WE'LL BE OUT ALL DAY TOMORROW, CAROLINE, LUVVY. WE'LL BE STAYING OVER WITH APRIL'S NIECE IN ROYAL TUNBRIDGE WELLS.

THEY SHOWED CORALINE AN ALBUM WITH PHOTOS OF MISS SPINK'S NIECE IN IT.

THEN CORALINE LEFT...

...AND WALKED DOWN TO THE SUPER-MARKET.

SHE BOUGHT TWO BOTTLES OF LIMEADE, A CHOCOLATE CAKE, AND A NEW BAG OF APPLES...

...WENT BACK HOME...

...AND ATE THEM FOR DINNER.

SHE RAN HERSELF A BATH WITH TOO MUCH BUBBLE IN IT...

...DRIED HERSELF AND THE FLOOR AS BEST SHE COULD...

...AND WENT TO BED.

CORALINE WOKE UP IN THE NIGHT.

SHE WENT INTO HER PARENTS' BEDROOM BUT THE BED WAS MADE AND EMPTY.

AM 3:12

ALL ALONE, IN THE MIDDLE OF THE NIGHT, CORALINE BEGAN TO CRY. THERE WAS NO OTHER SOUND IN THE EMPTY FLAT.

SHE CLIMBED INTO HER PARENTS' BED, AND, AFTER A WHILE, SHE WENT TO SLEEP.

THE CAT WALKED THE LENGTH OF THE HALL AND STOPPED BY THE FULL-LENGTH MIRROR. IT HAD ONCE BEEN THE INSIDE OF A WARDROBE DOOR AND HAD BEEN HANGING THERE ON THE WALL WHEN THEY MOVED IN.

MUMMY AND DADDY!

REFLECTED IN THE MIRROR WERE HER PARENTS, SAD AND ALONE. HER FATHER SAID SOMETHING, BUT SHE COULD HEAR NOTHING AT ALL.

HER MOTHER BREATHED ON THE INSIDE OF THE MIRROR GLASS, AND QUICKLY, BEFORE THE FOG FADED, SHE WROTE...

THEY AREN'T GOING TO COME BACK, ARE THEY? NOT UNDER THEIR OWN STEAM.

THE CAT BLINKED AT HER.

RIGHT...

AH, THE NEFARIOUS CLUTCHES OF HER FIENDISH FINGERS, IS IT? MM. YOU KNOW WHAT I SUGGEST, MISS JONES?

NO. WHAT?

YOU ASK YOUR MOTHER TO MAKE YOU A BIG OLD MUG OF HOT CHOCOLATE, AND THEN GIVE YOU A GREAT BIG OLD HUG.

THERE'S NOTHING LIKE HOT CHOCOLATE AND A HUG FOR MAKING NIGHTMARES GO AWAY.

AND IF SHE STARTS TO TELL YOU OFF FOR WAKING HER UP AT THIS TIME OF NIGHT, WHY YOU TELL HER THAT THAT'S WHAT THE POLICEMAN SAID.

HE HAD A DEEP, REASSURING VOICE.

CORALINE WAS NOT REASSURED.

WHEN I SEE HER I SHALL TELL HER THAT.

CLICK

THE BLACK CAT, WHO HAD SAT ON THE FLOOR, GROOMING ITS FUR, THROUGH THIS ENTIRE CONVERSATION NOW STOOD UP AND LED THE WAY INTO THE HALL.

CORALINE WENT INTO THE KITCHEN AND FOUND A BOX OF EMERGENCY WHITE CANDLES...

...PUT AN APPLE INTO EACH POCKET...

...AND TOOK THE OLD BLACK KEY OFF THE RING.

BACK IN HER BED-ROOM SHE RUM-MAGED IN THE POCKET OF HER JEANS...

...FOUND THE STONE WITH THE HOLE IN IT...

...PUT IT INTO HER POCKET...

...AND WALKED INTO THE DRAWING ROOM.

SHE HAD THE FEELING THAT THE DOOR WAS LOOKING AT HER, WHICH SHE KNEW WAS SILLY, AND KNEW ON A DEEPER LEVEL WAS SOMEHOW TRUE.

WHEN I WAS A LITTLE GIRL, WHEN WE LIVED IN OUR OLD HOUSE, A LONG, LONG TIME AGO, MY DAD TOOK ME FOR A WALK ON THE WASTELAND BETWEEN OUR HOUSE AND THE SHOPS.

"IT WASN'T THE BEST PLACE TO GO FOR A WALK, REALLY. THERE WERE SHARP THINGS BACK THERE AND MUM SAID THERE WAS TETANUS AND SUCH."

BUT I KEPT TELLING THEM I WANTED TO EXPLORE IT.

"SO ONE DAY WE PUT ON OUR BOOTS AND GLOVES AND WE WENT FOR A WALK.

"WE WENT DOWN THIS HILL TO THE BOTTOM OF A GULLY WHEN MY DAD SAID SUDDENLY TO ME...

CORALINE—RUN AWAY. UP THE HILL. *NOW!*

"THE AIR WAS ALIVE WITH YELLOW WASPS. MY DAD STAYED AND GOT STUNG TO GIVE ME TIME TO RUN AWAY.

"HIS GLASSES HAD FALLEN OFF WHEN HE RAN.

"I ONLY HAD THE ONE STING ON THE BACK OF MY ARM. HE HAD THIRTY-NINE STINGS ALL OVER HIM.

AND SOON HE GOT HOME, WEARING HIS GLASSES.

"SO LATER THAT AFTERNOON MY DAD WENT BACK AGAIN TO THE WASTELAND TO GET HIS GLASSES BACK. HE SAID IF HE LEFT IT ANOTHER DAY HE WOULDN'T BE ABLE TO REMEMBER WHERE THEY'D FALLEN."

"HE SAID HE WASN'T SCARED WHEN HE WAS STANDING THERE AND THE WASPS WERE STINGING HIM AND HE WAS WATCHING ME RUN AWAY. BECAUSE HE KNEW HE HAD TO GIVE ME TIME TO RUN, OR THE WASPS WOULD HAVE COME AFTER BOTH OF US."

CLUNK

THE DOOR SWUNG OPEN.

AND HE SAID THAT WASN'T BRAVE OF HIM, JUST STANDING THERE AND BEING STUNG.

IT WASN'T BRAVE BECAUSE HE WASN'T SCARED. IT WAS THE ONLY THING HE COULD DO.

BUT GOING BACK AGAIN TO GET HIS GLASSES, WHEN HE KNEW THE WASPS WERE THERE, WHEN HE WAS REALLY SCARED. *THAT* WAS BRAVE.

AND WHY WAS THAT?

BECAUSE WHEN YOU'RE SCARED BUT YOU STILL DO IT ANYWAY, *THAT'S* BRAVE.

CORALINE HEARD SOMETHING MOVING IN THE DARKNESS. IT SEEMED TO BE KEEPING PACE WITH HER, WHATEVER IT WAS.

DON'T BE SILLY. I'M GOING BACK FOR THEM BECAUSE THEY ARE MY PARENTS.

YOU KNOW YOU'RE TALKING AGAIN?

AND THAT'S WHY YOU'RE GOING BACK TO HER WORLD, THEN? BECAUSE YOUR FATHER ONCE SAVED YOU FROM WASPS?

AND IF THEY NOTICED I WAS GONE I'M SURE THEY WOULD DO THE SAME FOR ME.

HOW FORTUNATE I AM IN HAVING A TRAVELING COMPANION OF SUCH WISDOM AND INTELLI-GENCE.

HHSS...

SHE WAS GOING TO SAY SOME-THING SARCASTIC IN RETURN LIKE...

SORRY...

...WHEN...

FSSST

...THERE WAS A SCRABBLING AND A PATTERING AND CORALINE COULD FEEL HER HEART POUNDING AGAINST HER RIBS.

SHE PUT OUT ONE HAND... AND FELT SOMETHING WISPY, LIKE A SPIDER'S WEB, BRUSH HER HANDS AND HER FACE.

AT THE END OF THE CORRIDOR THE ELECTRIC LIGHT WENT ON, BLINDING AFTER THE DARKNESS.

CORALINE?

DARLING?

MUM!

DARLING...

...WHY DID YOU EVER RUN AWAY FROM ME?

CORALINE WAS TOO CLOSE TO STOP, AND SHE FELT THE OTHER MOTHER'S COLD ARMS ENFOLD HER.

WHERE ARE MY PARENTS?

WE'RE **HERE**, READY TO LOVE YOU AND FEED YOU AND MAKE YOUR LIFE INTEREST-ING.

COME ON INTO THE KITCHEN. I'LL MAKE US A MIDNIGHT SNACK. HOT CHOCOLATE, PERHAPS?

C ORALINE PULLED AWAY FROM THE OTHER MOTHER, LEFT THE DRAWING ROOM, AND PASSED BEFORE THE MIRROR IN THE HALLWAY.

THERE WAS NOTHING REFLECTED IN IT BUT A YOUNG GIRL WHO LOOKED LIKE SHE HAD BEEN CRYING, BUT WHOSE EYES WERE REAL EYES, NOT BLACK BUTTONS.

I WILL BE BRAVE.

NO, I **AM** BRAVE!

I DON'T NEED A SNACK. I HAVE AN APPLE...

...SEE?

THE OTHER FATHER LOOKED DISAP-POINTED.

THE OTHER MOTHER SMILED, AND EACH OF HER TEETH WAS A TINY BIT TOO LONG.

...AND THEN IT CLEARED AND CORALINE WAS LOOKING AT THE HALLWAY ALL THE WAY DOWN TO THE FRONT DOOR AS IT OPENED.

THAT WAS A FINE HOLIDAY.

HOW NICE IT IS NOT TO HAVE CORALINE ANYMORE.

NOW WE CAN DO ALL THE THINGS WE ALWAYS WANTED TO DO, LIKE GO ABROAD, BUT WERE PREVENTED FROM DOING BY HAVING A LITTLE DAUGHTER.

AND I TAKE GREAT COMFORT IN KNOWING THAT HER OTHER MOTHER WILL TAKE BETTER CARE OF HER THAN WE EVER COULD.

THE MIRROR FOGGED AND FADED ONCE MORE.

SEE?

NO, I **DON'T** SEE. AND I DON'T BELIEVE IT EITHER.

BUT THERE WAS A TINY DOUBT INSIDE HER, LIKE A MAGGOT IN AN APPLE CORE. THEN SHE SAW THE EXPRESSION ON HER OTHER MOTHER'S FACE: A FLASH OF REAL ANGER, AND CORALINE KNEW THAT WHAT SHE HAD SEEN IN THE MIRROR WAS NO MORE THAN AN ILLUSION.

AND THEN THE CAT WAS GONE.

STILL... HE HAS A POINT.

SHE CREPT BACK INTO THE SILENT HOUSE...

...AND PASSED THE CLOSED BEDROOM DOOR INSIDE WHICH THE OTHER MOTHER... WHAT?
SLEPT?
WAITED?

AND THEN IT CAME TO HER...

IT'S AN *EMPTY* ROOM AND IT WILL REMAIN EMPTY UNTIL THE EXACT MOMENT THAT I OPEN THE DOOR.

SOMEHOW THAT MADE IT EASIER, THOUGH SHE STILL CHECKED FOR RATS UNDER HER OTHER BED.

NOTHING HERE.

SHE CLIMBED INTO BED AND FELL ASLEEP WITH BARELY ENOUGH TIME TO REFLECT, AS SHE DID SO, ON WHAT THE CAT COULD HAVE MEANT BY...

A CHALLENGE...

6

CORALINE WAS WOKEN BY THE MID-MORNING SUN ON HER FACE. FOR A MOMENT SHE FELT UTTERLY DISLOCATED.

AND THEN THE GREEN AND PINKNESS OF THE ROOM SHE WAS IN, AND THE RUSTLING OF A LARGE PAPER BUTTERFLY, TOLD HER WHERE SHE HAD WOKEN UP.

I CAN'T WEAR MY PAJAMAS DURING THE DAY...

...THAT MEANS WEARING THE OTHER CORALINE'S CLOTHES.

IS THERE ANOTHER CORALINE?

NO. THERE'S JUST *ME*.

THERE WERE NO REGULAR CLOTHES IN THE CUPBOARD, THOUGH. THEY WERE MORE LIKE DRESSING-UP CLOTHES...OR COSTUMES.

FINALLY SHE FOUND A PAIR OF JEANS, A SWEATER...

...AND A PAIR OF BOOTS.

FROM OUT OF HER POCKET SHE TOOK HER LAST APPLE AND THE STONE WITH A HOLE IN IT.

SHE PUT THE STONE BACK INTO HER POCKET AND IT WAS AS IF HER HEAD HAD CLEARED A LITTLE...

...LIKE COMING OUT OF A FOG.

SHE WENT INTO THE KITCHEN, BUT IT WAS DESERTED.

STILL, SHE WAS SURE THAT THERE WAS SOMEONE IN THE FLAT. SHE WALKED DOWN THE HALL.

THE OTHER FATHER WAS SITTING AT A DESK JUST LIKE HER FATHER'S, BUT HE WAS ONLY PRETENDING TO BE WORKING.

WHERE'S THE OTHER MOTHER?

OUT. FIXING THE DOORS. THERE ARE SOME VERMIN PROBLEMS.

THE RATS, YOU MEAN?

NO, THE RATS ARE OUR FRIENDS. THIS IS THE OTHER KIND. BIG BLACK FELLOW WITH HIS TAIL HIGH.

THE CAT, YOU MEAN?

THAT'S THE ONE.

HE LOOKED LESS LIKE HER TRUE FATHER TODAY. THERE WAS SOMETHING SLIGHTLY VAGUE ABOUT HIS FACE—LIKE BREAD DOUGH THAT HAD BEGUN TO RISE.

I SHALL DEMONSTRATE OUR TENDER HOSPITALITY TO YOU, SUCH THAT YOU WILL NOT EVEN THINK ABOUT EVER GOING BACK.

REALLY, I MUSTN'T TALK TO YOU WHEN SHE ISN'T HERE.

BUT DON'T YOU WORRY, SHE WON'T BE GONE OFTEN.

SO, WHAT AM I TO DO NOW?

SHHHHH.

IF YOU WON'T EVEN TALK TO ME, I AM GOING EXPLORING.

NO POINT.

THIS IS ALL SHE MADE: THE HOUSE, THE GROUNDS, AND THE PEOPLE IN THE HOUSE. SHE MADE IT...

THERE ISN'T ANYWHERE BUT *HERE.*

...AND SHE WAITED.

SHHHH.

BUT HOW...?

SHE WENT INTO THE DRAWING ROOM, OVER TO THE OLD DOOR, AND SHE PULLED ON IT.

RATS! IT'S LOCKED FAST...

...AND THE OTHER MOTHER HAS THE KEY.

SHE LOOKED AROUND THE ROOM. IT WAS SO FAMILIAR—THAT WAS WHAT MADE IT FEEL SO TRULY STRANGE. EVERYTHING WAS EXACTLY THE SAME AS SHE REMEMBERED...

...BUT THERE WAS SOMETHING ELSE...

...SOMETHING SHE DID NOT REMEMBER SEEING BEFORE.

A BALL OF GLASS, UP ON THE MANTELPIECE.

A SNOW GLOBE WITH TWO LITTLE PEOPLE IN IT.

CORALINE SHOOK IT AND SET THE SNOW FLYING, WHITE SNOW THAT GLITTERED AS IT TUMBLED THROUGH THE WATER.

THEN SHE PUT THE SNOW GLOBE BACK ON THE MANTEL-PIECE AND CARRIED ON LOOKING FOR HER TRUE PARENTS...

...AND A WAY OUT.

SHE WENT OUT OF THE FLAT. PAST THE FLASHING-LIGHTS DOOR BEHIND WHICH THE OTHER MISSES SPINK AND FORCIBLE PERFORMED THEIR SHOW FOREVER...

...AND SHE SET OFF INTO THE WOODS.

WHERE CORALINE CAME FROM, ONCE YOU WERE THROUGH THE PATCH OF TREES YOU SAW NOTHING BUT THE MEADOW AND THE OLD TENNIS COURT.

IN THIS PLACE, THE WOODS WENT ON FARTHER, THE TREES BECOMING CRUDER THE FARTHER YOU WENT.

PRETTY SOON THEY SEEMED VERY APPROXIMATE, LIKE THE IDEA OF TREES.

SHE KEPT WALKING. AND THEN THE MIST BEGAN. IT WAS NOT DAMP, LIKE A NORMAL FOG OR MIST. IT WAS NOT COLD AND IT WAS NOT WARM. IT FELT TO CORALINE LIKE SHE WAS WALKING INTO NOTHING.

I'M AN EXPLORER.

AND I NEED ALL THE WAYS OUT OF HERE I CAN GET.

SO I SHALL KEEP WALKING.

THE WORLD SHE WAS WALKING THROUGH WAS A PALE NOTHINGNESS, LIKE A BLANK SHEET OF PAPER. IT HAD NO SMELL, TEXTURE, OR TASTE.

IT CERTAINLY ISN'T MIST.

AND WHAT DO YOU THINK YOU'RE DOING HERE?

SHE THOUGHT IT MIGHT BE SOME KIND OF LION, AT FIRST, SOME DISTANCE AWAY FROM HER.

AND THEN SHE KNEW WHAT IT WAS.

I'M EX-PLORING.

BAD PLACE FOR EXPLOR-ING.

NOTHING TO FIND HERE.

THIS IS JUST THE OUTSIDE, THE PART OF THE PLACE *SHE* HASN'T BOTHERED TO CREATE...THE ONE WHO SAYS SHE'S YOUR OTHER MOTHER.

WHAT *IS* SHE?

THE CAT DID NOT ANSWER.

NO! WHY DO YOU DO IT? YOU'RE TORTURING IT.

MM...

...THERE ARE THOSE WHO HAVE SUGGESTED THAT THE TENDENCY OF A CAT TO PLAY WITH ITS PREY IS A MERCIFUL ONE.

AFTER ALL, IT PERMITS THE OCCASIONAL FUNNY LITTLE RUNNING SNACK TO ESCAPE FROM TIME TO TIME.

HOW OFTEN DOES *YOUR* DINNER GET TO ESCAPE?

AND THEN IT PICKED UP THE RAT IN ITS MOUTH AND CARRIED IT OFF INTO THE WOODS, BEHIND A TREE.

CORALINE WALKED BACK INTO THE HOUSE.

ALL WAS QUIET AND EMPTY AND DESERTED.

SHE COULD SEE HERSELF WALKING TOWARD THE MIRROR, LOOKING, REFLECTED, A LITTLE BRAVER THAN SHE ACTUALLY FELT.

« 86 »

WHO ARE YOU?

NAMES, NAMES, NAMES.

THE NAMES ARE THE FIRST THINGS TO GO.

WE KEEP OUR MEMORIES LONGER THAN OUR NAMES.

I REMEMBER MY GOVERNESS, AND THE MORNING SUN, AND ALL THE TULIPS BOBBING IN THE BREEZE. BUT I HAVE FORGOTTEN THE NAME OF THE GOVERNESS AND OF THE TULIPS, TOO.

I DON'T THINK TULIPS HAVE NAMES. THEY'RE JUST TULIPS.

PERHAPS.

BUT I ALWAYS THOUGHT TULIPS MUST HAVE NAMES.

THEY WERE RED AND ORANGE AND YELLOW...

...LIKE EMBERS IN THE NURSERY FIRE...

...I REMEMBER THEM.

THE VOICE SOUNDED SO SAD THAT CORALINE PUT OUT A HAND AND FOUND A COLD HAND IN RETURN. SHE SQUEEZED IT TIGHTLY.

THANK YOU.

HER EYES WERE BEGINNING TO GET USED TO THE DARKNESS AND SHE BEGAN TO DISCERN THREE SHAPES, CHILD-LIKE, AND PALE AS THE MOON.

ARE YOU A GIRL OR A BOY?

FLEE! FLEE WHILE THERE'S STILL AIR IN YOUR LUNGS...

...AND BLOOD IN YOUR VEINS...

...AND WARMTH IN YOUR HEART.

I'M NOT RUNNING AWAY.

SHE HAS MY PARENTS.

I CAME TO GET THEM BACK.

AH, BUT SHE'LL KEEP YOU HERE WHILE THE DAYS TURN TO DUST AND THE YEARS PASS ONE AFTER THE NEXT LIKE THE TICK-TICK-TOCKING OF A CLOCK.

NO!

SHE WON'T.

THERE WAS A SILENCE THEN IN THE ROOM BEHIND THE MIRROR.

PERADVENTURE, IF YOU COULD WIN YOUR MOMMA AND YOUR PAPA BACK FROM THE BELDAM, YOU COULD ALSO WIN FREE *OUR* SOULS.

HAS SHE TAKEN THEM?

AYE. AND HIDDEN THEM.

THAT IS WHY WE COULD NOT LEAVE HERE WHEN WE DIED. SHE KEPT US AND FED ON US, UNTIL NOW WE'VE NOTHING LEFT OF OURSELVES.

FIND OUR SECRET HEARTS, YOUNG MISTRESS.

THE OTHER MOTHER LOOKED HEALTHIER THAN BEFORE: THERE WAS A LITTLE BLUSH TO HER CHEEKS, AND HER HAIR WAS WRIGGLING LIKE LAZY SNAKES ON A WARM DAY. HER BLACK BUTTON EYES SEEMED FRESHLY POLISHED.

SHE HAD PUSHED THROUGH THE MIRROR AS IF SHE WERE WALKING THROUGH NOTHING MORE SOLID THAN WATER.

THEN SHE HAD OPENED THE DOOR WITH THE LITTLE SILVER KEY...

...PICKED CORALINE UP, CRADLING THE HALF-SLEEPING CHILD AS IF SHE WERE A BABY...

As she ate, her other mother stared at her. Coraline thought she looked hungry, too.

WHERE SHOULD I START LOOKING?

WHERE YOU WISH.

CORALINE THOUGHT HARD. THERE WAS NO POINT IN EXPLORING THE GARDEN AND THE GROUNDS: THEY DIDN'T EXIST; THEY WEREN'T REAL.

ALL THAT WAS REAL WAS THE HOUSE ITSELF.

SHE LOOKED AROUND THE KITCHEN.

SHE OPENED THE OVEN...

...PEERED INTO THE FREEZER...

WARNING

...POKED INTO THE SALAD COMPARTMENT.

THE OTHER MOTHER FOLLOWED HER ABOUT, LOOKING AT CORALINE WITH A SMIRK ALWAYS HOVERING AT THE EDGE OF HER LIPS.

HOW BIG ARE SOULS ANYWAY?

MMM.

TAP TAP TAP TAP

SHE PUT HER HAND INTO HER POCKET...

...AND WALKED INTO THE HALL.

SHE GLANCED AT THE MIRROR AT THE END OF THE HALL...

...AND FOR A MOMENT IT SEEMED TO HER THAT FACES SWAM IN THE GLASS.

TAP TAP TAP

THEN THE FACES WERE GONE, AND THERE WAS NOTHING IN THE MIRROR BUT A GIRL WHO WAS SMALL FOR HER AGE HOLDING SOMETHING THAT GLOWED GENTLY, LIKE A GREEN COAL.

HMM.

A TRAIL OF GREEN FIRE BLEW FROM THE STONE IN THE MIRROR AND DRIFTED TOWARD CORALINE'S BEDROOM.

THE TOYS FLUTTERED EXCITEDLY AS IF THEY WERE HAPPY TO SEE HER.

SHE LOOKED AROUND THE ROOM...

...IN THE CUPBOARDS AND THE DRAWERS...

?

...AND IN THE TOY BOX.

NONE OF THE TOYS LOOKED PARTICULARLY SOUL-LIKE.

THEN SHE REMEM-BERED A VOICE...

...A VOICE IN THE DARKNESS.

LOOK THROUGH THE STONE.

IF I'M GOING TO DO THIS, I'M NOT GOING TO DO IT IN HER CLOTHES.

SHE CHANGED BACK INTO HER PAJAMAS, PUT THE MARBLE INTO HER DRESSING GOWN POCKET AND WALKED OUT INTO THE HALL.

SOMETHING STUNG HER FACE AND HANDS LIKE SAND BLOWING ON A BEACH. IT WAS A VICIOUS WIND, AND A COLD ONE.

THE GHOST VOICE WHISPERED TO HER...

OH, KEEP GOING FOR THE BELDAM IS ANGRY. SHE SENDS THIS WIND.

PLAY FAIR!

THERE WAS NO REPLY. BUT THE WIND WHIPPED ABOUT HER ONE MORE TIME, PETULANTLY, AND THEN IT DROPPED AWAY...

...AND WAS GONE.

OH!

CORALINE SCANNED THE ROOM, LOOKING FOR A TELLTALE SIGN THAT SOMEWHERE IN THIS ROOM WAS ANOTHER HIDDEN SOUL.

THERE WAS SOMETHING UP ON THE BACK WALL BEHIND THE RUINED STAGE. IT WAS GRAYISH WHITE, TWICE THE SIZE OF CORALINE HER-SELF, AND IT WAS STUCK TO THE WALL LIKE A SLUG.

PERHAPS THERE ARE NO SOULS HIDDEN IN HERE. PERHAPS I CAN JUST LEAVE AND GO SOME-WHERE ELSE.

BUT SOMETHING GLOWED INSIDE THE SAC.

CORALINE TRIED TO MAKE AS LITTLE NOISE AS SHE COULD...

...AFRAID THAT IF SHE DISTURBED THE THING IN THE SAC...

...IT WOULD OPEN ITS EYES...

...AND SEE HER...

...AND THEN...

...THEN SHE PUSHED HER HAND INTO THE STICKY CLINGING WHITENESS OF THE STUFF ON THE WALL.

IT CRACKLED SOFTLY, LIKE A TINY FIRE. SHE REACHED UPWARD TOWARD A COLD HAND CLOSED TIGHTLY AROUND ANOTHER GLASS MARBLE.

CORALINE TUGGED AT IT.

AT FIRST, NOTHING HAPPENED. THEN, ONE BY ONE THE FINGERS LOOSENED THEIR GRIP...

...AND THE MARBLE SLIPPED INTO HER HAND.

SHE PULLED HER ARM BACK THROUGH THE STICKY WEBBING, RELIEVED THAT THE THING'S EYES HAD NOT OPENED.

THEIR FACES RESEMBLED, SHE DECIDED, YOUNGER VERSIONS OF MISS SPINK AND MISS FORCIBLE, BUT TWISTED AND SQUEEZED TOGETHER, LIKE TWO LUMPS OF WAX, MELTED TOGETHER INTO ONE GHASTLY THING.

THE AIR BECAME ALIVE WITH DOG-BATS. CORALINE REALIZED THEN THAT, TERRIFYING THOUGH THE THING ON THE WALL THAT HAD ONCE BEEN THE OTHER MISSES SPINK AND FORCIBLE WAS, IT WAS ATTACHED TO THE WALL BY ITS WEB.

IT COULD NOT FOLLOW HER.

FLEE, MISS! FLEE NOW! YOU HAVE TWO OF US!

FLEE THIS PLACE WHILE YOUR BLOOD STILL FLOWS!

CORALINE DROPPED THE MARBLE IN HER POCKET AND RAN FOR THE DOOR.

DESPITE HERSELF, CORALINE NODDED. IT WAS TRUE.

AS A MISER LOVES MONEY, OR A DRAGON LOVES ITS GOLD.

I DON'T WANT YOUR LOVE. I DON'T WANT ANYTHING FROM YOU.

NOT EVEN A LITTLE HINT?

I'M DOING FINE ON MY OWN.

YES. BUT IF YOU WANTED TO GET INTO THE FLAT IN THE FRONT—THE EMPTY ONE—TO LOOK AROUND, YOU WOULD FIND THE DOOR LOCKED, AND THEN WHERE WOULD YOU BE?

OH...

...IS THERE A KEY?

HAK HAK

HERE. YOU'LL NEED THIS TO GET IN.

EEEEW.

SHE WALKED THROUGH THE EMPTY KITCHEN...

...PAST THE EMPTY BATHROOM. IN THE TUB WAS A DEAD SPIDER THE SIZE OF A SMALL CAT.

THEN, WALKING THROUGH AN EMPTY BEDROOM, SHE SAW SOMETHING...

A TRAP-DOOR?!

UP THROUGH THE HOLE CAME THE SMELL OF DAMP CLAY, AND SOMETHING ELSE.

SOUR VINEGAR.

CORALINE LOOKED AT THE CELLAR THROUGH THE STONE WITH THE HOLE IN IT BUT SAW NOTHING.

SHE LET HERSELF DOWN INTO THE HOLE, LOOKING NERVOUSLY AT THE TRAPDOOR. IT WAS SO HEAVY THAT IF IT FELL SHE WAS SURE SHE WOULD BE TRAPPED IN THE DARKNESS FOREVER.

AND THEN SHE WALKED DOWN THE STEPS.

THE BAD SMELL WAS WORSE NOW.

SHE WAS READY TO TURN AND LEAVE...

...WHEN SHE SAW...

IGGK.

AS IF IT HAD HEARD HER THE THING BEGAN TO SIT UP, AND IN A VOICE THAT NO LONGER EVEN FAINTLY RESEMBLED HER FATHER,

WHISPERED...

CORALINE

THE THING NODDED, AND AS IT DID...

...THE LEFT BUTTON EYE FELL OFF.

THE THING LOOKED AROUND VACANTLY WITH ITS ONE EYE AS IF IT HAD LOST HER.

RUN, CHILD. SHE WANTS ME TO KEEP YOU HERE FOREVER, SO THAT YOU CAN NEVER FINISH THE GAME AND SHE WILL WIN.

SHE IS PUSHING ME SO HARD TO HURT YOU. I CANNOT FIGHT HER.

YOU *CAN!* BE BRAVE!

ALAS...

...I CANNOT.

AND IT LUNGED TOWARD HER, ITS TOOTHLESS MOUTH WIDE OPEN.

CORALINE HAD A
SINGLE HEARTBEAT
IN WHICH TO REACT.
SHE COULD ONLY
THINK OF TWO THINGS
TO DO. EITHER SHE
COULD SCREAM AND
TRY TO RUN AWAY,
AND BE CHASED
AROUND A BADLY LIT
CELLAR BY THE
HUGE GRUB THING,
BE CHASED UNTIL
IT CAUGHT HER.
OR SHE COULD DO
SOMETHING ELSE.

SO SHE DID
SOMETHING
ELSE.

TAK   TAK   TIK

MY EYYYEEE!

THE TRAPDOOR CRASHED DOWN WITH A THUMP JUST AS SOMETHING LARGE BANGED AGAINST IT. IT SHOOK AND RATTLED IN THE FLOOR, BUT IT STAYED WHERE IT WAS.

CORALINE TOOK A DEEP BREATH AND WALKED OUT OF THE FLAT AS FAST AS SHE COULD, WITHOUT ACTUALLY RUNNING.

SHE HAD HALF EXPECTED THAT THE OTHER MOTHER WOULD BE WAITING FOR HER TO COME OUT, BUT THE WORLD WAS SILENT AND EMPTY. CORALINE WANTED TO GO HOME.

SHE TOLD HERSELF...

I'M BRAVE.

AND SHE ALMOST BELIEVED IT.

10

IT WAS TIME TO VISIT THE TOPMOST FLAT, WHERE, IN HER WORLD, THE CRAZY OLD MAN UPSTAIRS LIVED.

SHE HAD GONE UP THERE ONCE WITH HER REAL MOTHER COLLECTING FOR CHARITY.

THEY HAD STOOD IN THE DOORWAY WAITING FOR THE CRAZY OLD MAN. THE FLAT HAD SMELLED OF STRANGE FOODS AND PIPE TOBACCO AND ODD, SHARP CHEESY-SMELLING THINGS CORALINE COULD NOT NAME.

SHE HAD NOT WANTED TO GO ANY FARTHER INSIDE THAN THAT.

I'M AN EX-PLORER!

SHE SPOKE OUT LOUD, BUT HER WORDS SOUNDED MUFFLED AND DEAD ON THE MISTY AIR.

SHE HAD MADE IT OUT OF THE CELLAR, HADN'T SHE?

BUT IF THERE WAS ONE THING THAT CORALINE WAS CERTAIN OF, IT WAS THAT THIS FLAT WOULD BE WORSE.

IT SMELLED MUCH WORSE IN HERE THAN IN THE REAL CRAZY OLD MAN UPSTAIRS'S FLAT. THAT MERELY SMELLED OF EXOTIC FOOD. THIS PLACE SMELLED AS IF ALL THE EXOTIC FOODS IN THE WORLD HAD BEEN LEFT OUT TO GO ROTTEN.

UGH!

LITTLE GIRL...

YES?

I'M **NOT** FRIGHTENED.

AND AS SHE THOUGHT IT, SHE KNEW IT WAS TRUE.

THESE THINGS—EVEN THE THING IN THE CELLAR—WERE ILLUSIONS MADE BY THE OTHER MOTHER, WHO COULD NOT CREATE BUT ONLY TWIST AND COPY AND DISTORT THINGS THAT ALREADY EXISTED.

THEN SHE REMEMBERED THE SNOW GLOBE THE OTHER MOTHER HAD PLACED ON THE MANTEL-PIECE, AND SHE WONDERED...

WHY?

FOR THE MANTELPIECE IN CORALINE'S WORLD WAS QUITE BARE.

AND AS SOON AS SHE HAD ASKED HERSELF THE QUESTION, SHE KNEW THE ANSWER.

THEN THE VOICE CAME AGAIN, AND HER TRAIN OF THOUGHT WAS INTERRUPTED.

COME HERE, LITTLE GIRL.

IT WAS A RUSTLING VOICE. SCRATCHY AND DRY LIKE SOME KIND OF ENORMOUS DEAD INSECT.

WHICH WAS SILLY. HOW COULD A DEAD THING, ESPECIALLY A DEAD INSECT, HAVE A VOICE?

I KNOW WHAT YOU WANT, LITTLE GIRL.

THE HAIRS ON THE BACK OF CORALINE'S NECK PRICKLED. SHE KNEW THAT THE GIRL'S VOICE TOLD THE TRUTH.

SHE HAD ALL THREE MARBLES, NOW.

ALL SHE NEEDED TO DO WAS TO FIND HER PARENTS.

AND, CORALINE REALIZED WITH SURPRISE, SHE KNEW EXACTLY WHERE HER PARENTS WERE. AFTER ALL, THE MANTELPIECE IN THE DRAWING ROOM AT HOME WAS QUITE EMPTY.

BUT KNOWING THAT, SHE KNEW SOMETHING ELSE AS WELL...

THE OTHER MOTHER. SHE PLANS TO BREAK HER PROMISE. SHE WON'T LET US GO.

I WOULDN'T PUT IT PAST HER.

LIKE I SAID, THERE'S NO GUARANTEE SHE'LL PLAY FAIR.

HULLO... DID YOU SEE *THAT?*

WHAT?

LOOK BEHIND YOU.

THE HOUSE HAD FLATTENED OUT EVEN MORE. NOW IT SEEMED NO MORE THAN A CRUDE SCRIBBLE OF A HOUSE.

WHATEVER'S HAPPENING, THANK YOU FOR HELPING WITH THE RAT.

I SUPPOSE I'M ALMOST THERE, AREN'T I? SO YOU GO OFF INTO THE MIST, OR WHEREVER YOU GO, AND I'LL SEE YOU AT HOME.

IF SHE LETS ME GO HOME.

WHAT'S WRONG?

THEY'VE **GONE**. THEY AREN'T HERE ANYMORE. THE WAYS IN AND OUT OF THIS PLACE. THEY JUST WENT FLAT.

IS THAT **BAD?**

THE CAT MADE A LOW GROWLING NOISE IN THE BACK OF ITS THROAT AND BEGAN TO WALK BACKWARD STIFFLY, ONE STEP AT A TIME.

IT WAS TREMBLING LIKE A DEAD LEAF IN A STORM.

YOU'LL BE FINE. I'LL TAKE YOU HOME.

COME ON, CAT.

IF THE ONLY WAY OUT IS PAST HER, THEN THAT'S THE WAY WE'RE GOING TO GO.

THE CAT DID NOT RESIST. IT SIMPLY TREMBLED.

CORALINE WALKED UP THE STAIRS ONE AT A TIME, AWARE OF THE MARBLES CLICKING IN HER POCKET, THE STONE WITH A HOLE IN IT, AND THE CAT PRESSING ITSELF AGAINST HER.

SHE GOT TO HER FRONT DOOR— NOW JUST A CHILD'S SCRAWL— AND WENT THROUGH.

HER GRAND-MOTHER'S FORMAL FURNITURE WAS STILL THERE...

...AND AT THE END OF THE ROOM STOOD THE WOODEN DOOR THAT HAD ONCE, IN ANOTHER PLACE, OPENED ONTO A PLAIN BRICK WALL.

THE WINDOW SHOWED NOTHING BUT MIST.

THIS WAS IT, CORALINE KNEW. THE MOMENT OF TRUTH. THE UNRAVEL-ING TIME.

IT'S FUNNY. THE OTHER MOTHER DOESN'T LOOK ANY-THING AT ALL LIKE MY OWN MOTHER.

HOW COULD I EVER HAVE THOUGHT THERE WAS A RESEMBLANCE?

WELL? WHERE ARE THEY?

HOLD ON. WE AREN'T FINISHED YET, ARE WE?

THE OTHER MOTHER LOOKED DAGGERS, BUT SHE SMILED SWEETLY.

NO. I SUPPOSE NOT. YOU STILL NEED TO FIND YOUR PARENTS, DON'T YOU?

YES.

I MUST NOT LOOK AT THE MANTELPIECE.

I MUST NOT EVEN THINK ABOUT IT.

PRODUCE THEM!

WELL?

WOULD YOU LIKE TO LOOK IN THE CELLAR AGAIN? I HAVE SOME OTHER INTERESTING THINGS HIDDEN DOWN THERE, YOU KNOW.

NO.

I KNOW WHERE MY PARENTS ARE.

CORALINE CAREFULLY UNHOOKED THE CAT'S CLAWS FROM HER SHOULDER.

WHERE?

THE CAT SLASHED THE OTHER MOTHER'S CHEEK. BLOOD RAN FROM THE CUTS—NOT RED BLOOD, BUT A DEEP, TARRY BLACK STUFF.

THE CAT HISSED AND GAVE ONE LAST SCALPEL-SHARP SWIPE AT THE OTHER MOTHER'S FACE.

QUICKLY!

IT WAS COLDER IN THE CORRIDOR AND THE CAT HESITATED...

...THEN...

...IT RAN TO CORALINE.

SHUT!

COME ON, *PLEASE!*

CORALINE BEGAN TO PULL THE DOOR CLOSED. IT WAS HEAVIER THAN SHE IMAGINED A DOOR COULD BE, AND PULLING IT CLOSED WAS LIKE TRYING TO CLOSE A DOOR AGAINST A HIGH WIND. AND THEN SHE FELT SOMETHING STARTING TO PULL AGAINST HER.

THEY MOVED THROUGH HER, THEN; GHOST HANDS LENT HER STRENGTH THAT SHE NO LONGER POSSESSED.

THERE WAS A FINAL MOMENT OF RESISTANCE, AS IF SOMETHING WERE CAUGHT IN THE DOOR, AND THEN, WITH A **CRASH...**

...THE DOOR BANGED CLOSED.

SOMETHING DROPPED FROM CORALINE'S HEAD HEIGHT TO THE FLOOR. IT LANDED WITH A SORT OF SCUTTLING THUMP.

COME ON! THIS IS NOT A GOOD PLACE TO BE IN! **QUICKLY!**

CORALINE TURNED HER BACK ON THE DOOR AND BEGAN TO RUN THROUGH THE DARK CORRIDOR, SLIDING HER HAND ALONG THE WALL SO AS NOT TO GET TURNED AROUND IN THE DARKNESS.

AND THERE WAS SOMETHING ELSE...

...SCUTTLING BETWEEN HER FEET.

SHE CAUGHT HERSELF BEFORE SHE WENT DOWN.

SHE KNEW THAT IF SHE FELL IN THAT CORRIDOR SHE MIGHT NEVER GET UP AGAIN.

WHATEVER THAT CORRIDOR WAS WAS OLDER BY FAR THAN THE OTHER MOTHER. IT WAS DEEP, AND SLOW, AND IT KNEW THAT SHE WAS THERE...

ALMOST THERE...

BUT IN THE LIGHT SHE DISCOVERED THAT THE WRAITHS HAD GONE, AND SHE WAS ALONE.

SHE DID NOT HAVE TIME TO WONDER WHAT HAD HAPPENED TO THEM...

...AND SLAMMED THE DOOR BEHIND HER WITH THE LOUDEST, MOST SATISFYING **BANG** YOU CAN IMAGINE.

CLUNK

THE LIGHT THAT CAME THROUGH THE WINDOW WAS REAL GOLDEN LATE-AFTERNOON DAYLIGHT, NOT A WHITE MIST. THE ROBIN'S-EGG BLUE SKY HAD NEVER SEEMED SO *SKY*, THE WORLD HAD NEVER SEEMED SO *WORLD.*

THEN SHE LOOKED DOWN AT HER LAP AT THE WAY THE SUNLIGHT BRUSHED EVERY HAIR ON THE CAT'S HEAD.

NOTHING, SHE THOUGHT, HAD EVER BEEN SO *INTERESTING.*

AND, CAUGHT UP IN THE INTEREST-INGNESS OF THE WORLD, CORALIN BARELY NOTICED WHEN SHE FELL INTO A DEEP AND DREAMLESS SLEE

« 154 »

12

CORALINE? DARLING, WHAT A FUNNY PLACE TO FALL ASLEEP. AND REALLY, THIS ROOM IS ONLY FOR BEST. WE LOOKED ALL OVER THE HOUSE FOR YOU.

I CAN SEE THAT. AND WHEREVER DID THE CAT COME FROM? HE WAS WAITING BY THE FRONT DOOR. SHOT OUT LIKE A BULLET WHEN I CAME IN.

I'M SORRY. I FELL ASLEEP.

PROB- ABLY HAD THINGS TO DO.

THEN SHE HUGGED HER MOTHER SO TIGHTLY HER ARMS BEGAN TO ACHE.

DINNER IN FIFTEEN MINUTES. DON'T FORGET TO WASH YOUR HANDS. AND JUST *LOOK* AT THOSE PAJAMA BOTTOMS. WHAT DID YOU DO TO YOUR POOR KNEE?

AND SHE WENT INTO THE BATHROOM TO CLEAN HER CUTS AND SCRAPES.

I TRIPPED.

« 155 »

SHE WENT INTO HER BEDROOM— HER REAL BEDROOM, HER TRUE BEDROOM...

...AND EMPTIED HER POCKETS.

CORALINE WATCHED THE GLITTERY SNOW SWIRL THROUGH THE WATER TO FILL THE EMPTY WORLD, WATCHED THE SNOW FALL, COVERING THE PLACE WHERE THE LITTLE COUPLE HAD ONCE STOOD.

THE STONE WENT BACK INTO HER POCKET.

SHE WALKED TO HER FATHER'S STUDY. HE HAD HIS BACK TO HER, BUT SHE KNEW, JUST ON SEEING HIM, THAT HIS EYES, WHEN HE TURNED AROUND, WOULD BE HER FATHER'S KIND GRAY EYES.

HULLO. WHAT WAS THAT FOR?

NOTHING. I JUST MISS YOU SOME-TIMES.

THEN, FOR NO REASON AT ALL, HE PICKED CORALINE UP, WHICH HE HAD NOT DONE FOR SUCH A LONG TIME, NOT SINCE HE HAD STARTED POINTING OUT TO HER SHE WAS MUCH TOO OLD TO BE CARRIED, AND HE CARRIED HER INTO THE KITCHEN.

« 157 »

AND THEN, IN THE WAY OF DREAMS, THE PICNIC WAS DONE AND THEY WERE
PLAYING IN THE MEADOW, RUNNING AND SHOUTING AND TOSSING A
GLITTERING BALL FROM ONE TO ANOTHER. CORALINE KNEW IT
WAS A DREAM THEN, BECAUSE NONE OF THEM EVER GOT
TIRED OR WINDED OR OUT OF BREATH.

THANK YOU FOR COMING TO MY PARTY, IF IT *IS* MINE.

THE PLEASURE IS OURS, CORALINE JONES. IF THERE WERE BUT SOME-THING WE COULD DO FOR YOU TO THANK YOU AND TO REWARD YOU.

AYE.

IT'S A VERY FINE THING YOU DID FOR US, MISS.

WHEN THE GAME WAS DONE, THE FOUR OF THEM WENT BACK TO THE PICNIC CLOTH WHERE THERE WERE FOUR BOWLS WAITING FOR THEM, THREE OF ICE CREAM, ONE OF HONEYSUCKLE FLOWERS.

CORALINE STOOD IN THE MEADOW, AND SHE WATCHED AS THE THREE CHILDREN WENT AWAY FROM HER ACROSS THE GRASS.

AND WHAT CAME AFTER WAS DARKNESS.

SUDDENLY, SOMETHING DETACHED ITSELF FROM BENEATH THE BENCH AND MADE A MAD SCRABBLING DASH FOR THE DOOR.

EVEN AS IT CLICKED AND SCUTTLED PAST HER AND OUT OF THE HOUSE, SHE KNEW WHAT IT WAS AND WHAT IT WAS AFTER.

SHE HAD SEEN IT TOO MANY TIMES IN THE LAST FEW DAYS.

13

CORALINE'S PARENTS NEVER SEEMED TO REMEMBER ANYTHING ABOUT THEIR TIME IN THE SNOW GLOBE. SOMETIMES SHE WONDERED WHETHER THEY HAD EVER NOTICED THAT THEY HAD LOST TWO DAYS IN THE REAL WORLD. THEN AGAIN THERE ARE SOME PEOPLE WHO KEEP TRACK OF EVERY HOUR, AND THERE ARE PEOPLE WHO DON'T...

...AND CORALINE'S PARENTS WERE SOLIDLY IN THE SECOND CAMP.

CORALINE HAD PLACED THE MARBLES BENEATH HER PILLOW THAT FIRST NIGHT HOME.

SHE WENT BACK TO BED AFTER SHE SAW THE OTHER MOTHER'S HAND, AND AS SHE RESTED HER HEAD BACK ON THAT PILLOW...

...SOMETHING SCRUNCHED GENTLY.

THE FRAGMENTS OF THE GLASS MARBLES LOOKED LIKE THE REMAINS OF EGG-SHELLS ONE FINDS BENEATH TREES IN THE SPRING-TIME: LIKE EMPTY, BROKEN ROBINS' EGGS.

WHATEVER HAD BEEN IN THE GLASS SPHERES HAD GONE.

SHE GATHERED UP THE FRAGMENTS AND PLACED THEM IN A SMALL BOX THAT ONCE HELD A BRACELET HER GRAND-MOTHER HAD GIVEN HER.

THE BRACELET WAS LONG LOST...

...BUT THE BOX REMAINED.

MISS SPINK AND MISS FORCIBLE CAME BACK FROM VISITING MISS SPINK'S NIECE, AND CORALINE WENT DOWN TO THEIR FLAT FOR TEA.

IT WAS A MONDAY.

ON WEDNESDAY CORALINE WOULD GO BACK TO SCHOOL; A WHOLE NEW SCHOOL YEAR WOULD BEGIN.

MISS FORCIBLE INSISTED ON READING CORALINE'S TEA LEAVES.

WELL, LOOKS LIKE EVERYTHING'S MOSTLY SHIPSHAPE AND BRISTOL FASHION, LUVVY.

SORRY?

EVERYTHING'S COMING UP ROSES...

WELL, *ALMOST* EVERYTHING...

...I'M NOT SURE WHAT *THAT* IS.

HONESTLY, MIRIAM. GIVE IT OVER HERE. LET ME SEE...

A WHITE HAND WITH CRIMSON FINGER-NAILS LEAPT FROM THE WINDOW LEDGE ONTO A DRAINPIPE...

...AND WAS IMMEDIATELY OUT OF SIGHT.

THERE WERE DEEP GOUGES IN THE GLASS ON THE OTHER SIDE OF THE WINDOW.

CORALINE SLEPT UNEASILY THAT NIGHT, WAKING FROM TIME TO TIME TO PLOT AND PLAN AND PONDER, THEN FALLING BACK INTO SLEEP, NEVER QUITE CERTAIN WHERE HER PONDERING ENDED AND THE DREAM BEGAN.

ONE EAR ALWAYS OPEN FOR THE SOUND OF SOMETHING SCRATCHING AT HER WINDOW-PANE...

...OR AT HER BED-ROOM DOOR.

THE PLANKS COVERING THE WELL WERE ASTONISHINGLY HEAVY—ALMOST TOO HEAVY FOR A GIRL TO LIFT, BUT SHE MANAGED. SHE DIDN'T HAVE ANY CHOICE.

SHE CAREFULLY LAID THE TABLECLOTH ACROSS THE TOP OF THE WELL. SHE PLACED DOLL CUPS AROUND IT AND WEIGHED EACH CUP DOWN WITH WATER FROM THE JUG.

SHE PUT A DOLL IN THE GRASS BESIDE EACH CUP, MAKING IT LOOK AS MUCH LIKE A DOLLS' TEA PARTY AS SHE COULD

THEN SHE RE-TRACED HER STEPS.

♪

AND THEN THE WEIGHT AND THE MOMENTUM OF THE HAND SENT THE PLASTIC DOLLS' CUPS FLYING, AND THE PAPER TABLECLOTH, THE KEY, AND THE OTHER MOTHER'S RIGHT HAND WENT TUMBLING DOWN INTO THE DARKNESS OF THE WELL.

1 — 2 — 3 — 4 — 5   19 — 20 — 21 — 22 — 23 — 24   37 — 38 — 39 — 40 — ✳

PLOOSH

SHE HAULED THE HEAVY PLANKS BACK ONTO THE WELL, COVERING IT AS CAREFULLY AS SHE COULD. SHE DIDN'T WANT ANYTHING TO FALL IN.

SHE DIDN'T WANT ANYTHING TO EVER GET OUT.

AS SHE WAS COLLECTING HER DOLLS, SOMETHING CAUGHT HER EYE.

THE CAT ROLLED OVER ON ITS BACK AND CORALINE SCRATCHED AND TICKLED THE SOFT FUR ON ITS BELLY. THE CAT PURRED CONTENTEDLY.

THEN IT ROLLED OVER AND WALKED BACK TOWARD THE TENNIS COURT, LIKE A TINY PATCH OF MIDNIGHT IN THE MIDDAY SUN.

SHE KNOCKED AT MISS SPINK AND MISS FORCIBLE'S DOOR. MISS SPINK LET HER IN AND CORALINE WENT INTO THEIR PARLOR.

SHE PUT HER HAND INTO HER POCKET AND PULLED OUT THE STONE WITH THE HOLE IN IT.

HERE YOU GO.

I DON'T NEED IT ANY- MORE.

I'M VERY GRATE- FUL.

I THINK IT MAY HAVE SAVED MY LIFE, AND SAVED SOME OTHER PEOPLE'S DEATH.

SHE GAVE THEM BOTH TIGHT HUGS, ALTHOUGH HER ARMS BARELY STRETCHED AROUND MISS SPINK, AND MISS FORCIBLE SMELLED LIKE THE RAW GARLIC SHE HAD BEEN CUTTING.

WHAT AN EXTRA- ORDINARY CHILD.

THAT NIGHT CORALINE LAY IN BED. NOW THAT THE HAND WAS GONE SHE HAD OPENED HER WINDOW WIDE. HER NEW SCHOOL CLOTHES WERE LAID OUT CAREFULLY ON HER CHAIR.

NORMALLY, CORALINE WAS NERVOUS BEFORE THE FIRST DAY OF TERM BUT, SHE REALIZED...

THERE'S NOTHING LEFT ABOUT SCHOOL THAT CAN SCARE ME ANYMORE.

SHE FANCIED SHE COULD HEAR SWEET MUSIC ON THE NIGHT AIR—THE KIND OF MUSIC THAT CAN ONLY BE PLAYED ON THE TINIEST SILVER INSTRUMENTS.

SHE IMAGINED THAT SHE WAS BACK AGAIN IN HER DREAM WITH THE THREE CHILDREN.

As THE FIRST STARS CAME OUT, CORALINE FINALLY ALLOWED HERSELF TO DRIFT INTO SLEEP WHILE THE GENTLE UPSTAIRS MUSIC OF THE MOUSE CIRCUS SPILLED OUT ONTO THE WARM EVENING AIR, TELLING THE WORLD THAT THE SUMMER WAS ALMOST DONE.

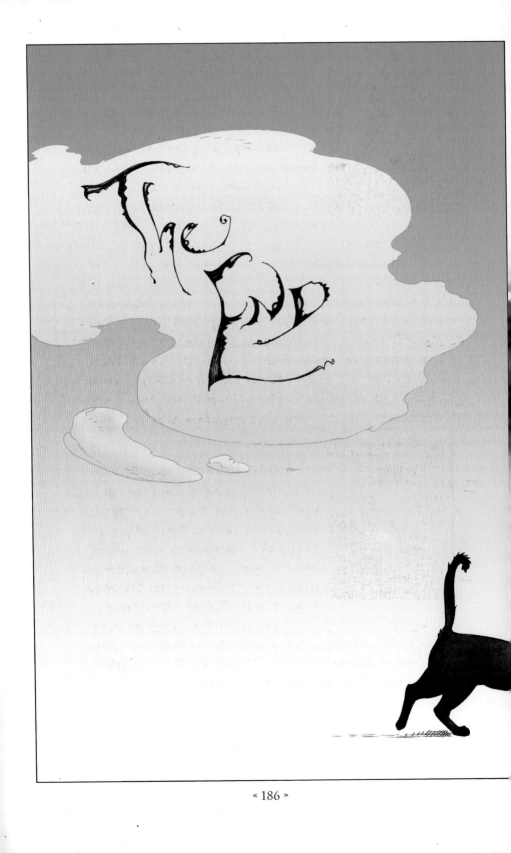